For my brother, Dave
–D.M.

From the television script "I Spy a Runaway Robot" by John Slama.
Based on the *I Spy* book series, written by Jean Marzollo and
photographed by Walter Wick.

Library of Congress Cataloging-in-Publication Data

Marzollo, Dan.
  I spy a runaway robot / by Dan Marzollo ; illustrated by Ward Yoshimoto.
      p. cm. -- (I spy)
"Cartwheel Books."
Summary: Characters locate a variety of hidden objects as they build a robot to help clean up their mess.
  ISBN 0-439-44318-0
  [1. Robots--Fiction. 2. Picture puzzles.]   I. Yoshimoto, Ward, ill.
  II. Title. III. Series: Marzollo, Dan. I spy.
  PZ7.M3688Ip 2003
  [E]--dc21
              2002009741

10 9 8 7 6 5 4 3 2 1   03 04 05 06 07

Printed in the U.S.A.
First printing, August 2003

A RUNAWAY ROBOT

by Dan Marzollo
Photographs by Ward Yoshimoto
and Studio 10/James Levin and Eric Philcox

SCHOLASTIC INC. Cartwheel B·O·O·K·S®

New York   Toronto   London   Auckland   Sydney
Mexico City   New Delhi   Hong Kong   Buenos Aires

"What a mess!"
said Spyler. "Who
will clean up?"

"Not me!" said CeCe.

"Not me, either!"
said Spyler. "I have
an idea. We'll build
a robot to clean up
for us!"

"What do we need
to make it?"
asked CeCe.

I spy!
You spy!
Let's all play
I Spy!

I spy a tin can,

A lightbulb for a head,

Two googly eyes,

And a bottle cap that's red.

"I spy a tin can!" said Spyler.

What rhymes with **can** that you can spy? Spyler and CeCe will wait while you try.

★ **frying pan**

★ **fan**

★ **man**

"I spy a lightbulb for a head!" said CeCe.

★ ★ ★ ★ ★ ★ ★

What other **round things** can you spy?
Spyler and CeCe
will wait while you try.

★ **red ball**

★ **clock**

★ **teacup**

"I spy two googly eyes!" said CeCe.

★ ★ ★ ★ ★ ★

What other **pairs**
can you spy?
Spyler and CeCe
will wait while you try.

★ **dice**

★ **socks**

★ **shoes**

"I spy a bottle cap that's red!" said Spyler.

★ ★ ★ ★ ★ ★ ★

What other **red things** can you spy?
Spyler and CeCe
will wait while you try.

★ hat

★ apple

★ glasses

3925299

15

"I have a tin can,
a lightbulb for the head,
two googly eyes,
and a bottle cap
that's red," said Spyler.

"Are you making our
robot?" asked CeCe.

"Yes, his name is
Clankenspy!" said
Spyler. "Here he
comes!"

"And there he goes!" said CeCe.

"Uh-oh," said Spyler. "He's knocking everything down! Push the red button, CeCe! That will make him stop!"

**Clankenspy stopped.
Spyler and CeCe
cleaned up the mess.**

★ ★ ★ ★ ★ ★ ★

For extra fun,
go back and look
for these **three objects**
hidden in this book.

★ **the letter Y**

★ **yo-yo**

★ **safety pin**

Then Clankenspy
made everyone tea
and cookies.

And they all enjoyed themselves
in their nice, clean home!